P9-DXH-041

CALGARY PUBLIC LIBRARY

DEC   2018

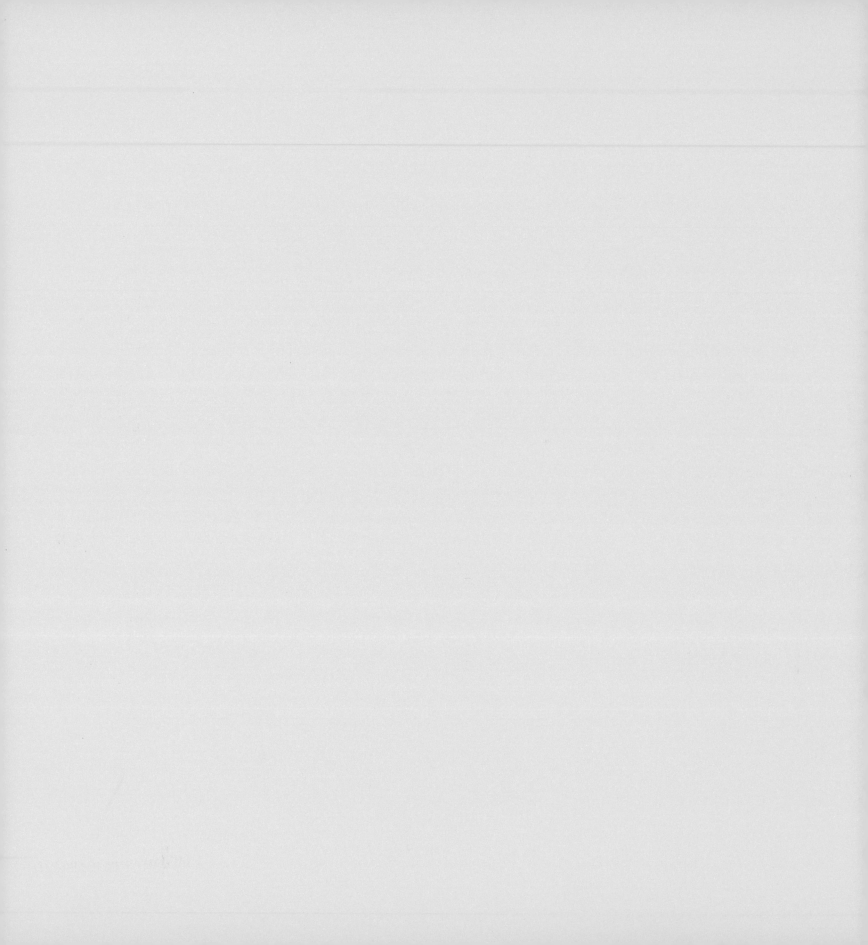

DON'T CALL ME BEAR!

Aaron Blabey

Scholastic Canada Ltd.
Toronto New York London Auckland Sydney
Mexico City New Delhi Hong Kong Buenos Aires

G'day, my name is **WARREN**

and I've got something to share . . .

Just because I'm furry

DOESN'T MEAN THAT I'M A BEAR.

Fig A
*Captain James Cook's
first sighting of a Koala*

and as he looked high into the towering eucalyptus, Captain Cook spied a small portly animal covered in a thick layer of fur and cried "Hey! A bear!"

Esteemed botanist Sir Joseph Banks stepped forward and declared, "Captain, I believe that is in fact a 'Koala,'" to which Captain Cook replied, "Yeah, yeah, whatevs" and went off in search of a flagon of rum.

his breeches, plucked a weevil fro

'Let's set up camp, Bank

THOSE SILLY PIONEERS!

CHART of COMMON MARSUPIALS

Possum Kangaroo Wombat Koala Tasma
Dev

See, if they'd done their homework,

then they'd know it wasn't true.
MARSUPIALS is what we are
and **YOU** should know that too.

So, I have had a gutful!

And I'm sorry if I shout —

I'M NOT A BEAR! I'M REALLY NOT!
AND YOU NEED TO
SORT IT OUT!

Kangaroos are
KANGAROOS.

You don't call
EMUS "chicks."

A **PLATYPUS**

is not a duck,

and I'm not playing tricks.

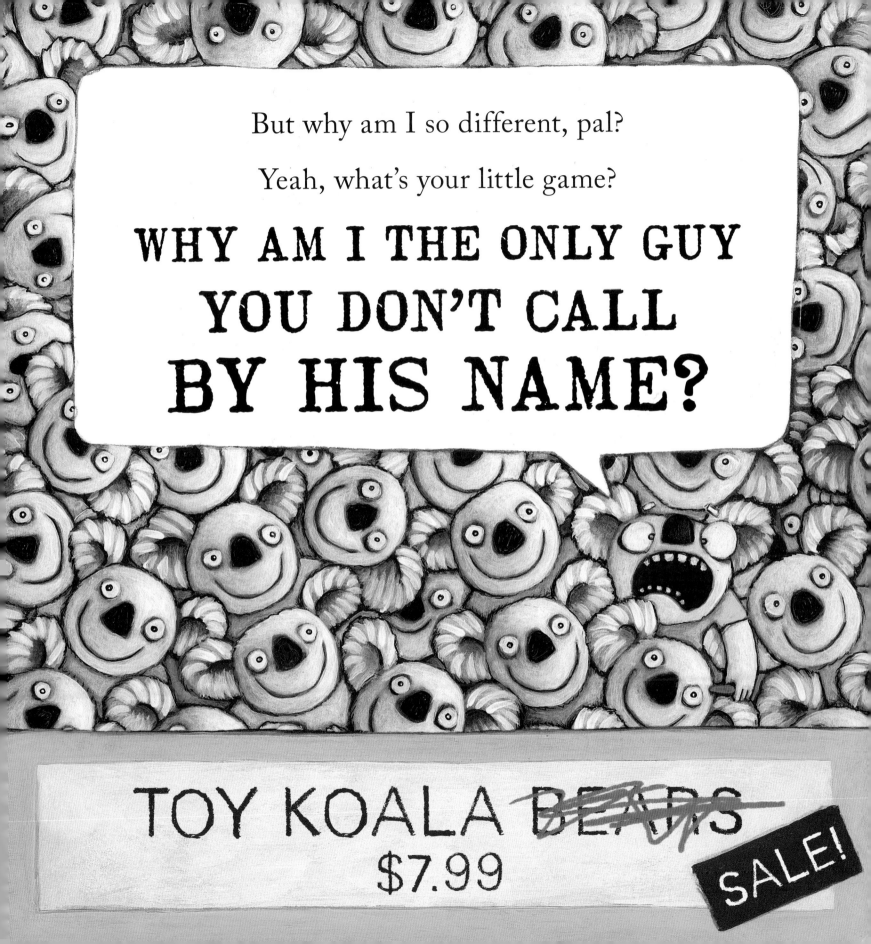

You may not be a bear, friend,

But you look like one, though . . .

For the F.W.C.M.Q.

Scholastic Canada Ltd.
604 King Street West, Toronto, Ontario M5V 1E1, Canada

Scholastic Inc.
557 Broadway, New York, NY 10012, USA

Scholastic Australia Pty Limited
PO Box 579, Gosford, NSW 2250, Australia

Scholastic New Zealand Limited
Private Bag 94407, Botany, Manukau 2163, New Zealand

Scholastic Children's Books
Euston House, 24 Eversholt Street, London NW1 1DB, UK

www.scholastic.ca

The artwork in this book is acrylic (with pens and pencils) on watercolour paper.
Typeset in Adobe Caslon and Incoming Fax.

Library and Archives Canada Cataloguing in Publication

Blabey, Aaron, author, illustrator
Don't call me bear! / Aaron Blabey.

Previously published: Gosford, NSW: Scholastic Press, 2016.
ISBN 978-1-4431-6395-8 (hardcover)

1. Stories in rhyme. I. Title. II. Title: Do not call me bear!.

PZ7.B529Don 2018   j823'.92   C2018-901501-2

First published by Scholastic Australia in 2017.
This edition published by Scholastic Canada in 2018.
Text and illustrations copyright © 2017 by Aaron Blabey.

All rights reserved.

No part of this publication may be reproduced or stored in a retrieval system, or transmitted in any form or by any means, electronic, mechanical, recording, or otherwise, without written permission of the publisher, Scholastic Canada Ltd., 604 King Street West, Toronto, Ontario M5V 1E1, Canada. In the case of photocopying or other reprographic copying, a licence must be obtained from Access Copyright (Canadian Copyright Licensing Agency), 56 Wellesley Street West, Suite 320, Toronto, Ontario M5S 2S3 (1-800-893-5777).

7 6 5 4 3 2   Printed in China   LFA   18 19 20 21 22 23